The Adirondack Kids® #8

Escape from Black Bear Mountain

The Adirondack Kids® #8

Escape from Black Bear Mountain

By Justin & Gary VanRiper
Illustrations by Carol VanRiper

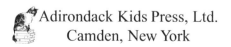
Adirondack Kids Press, Ltd.
Camden, New York

The Adirondack Kids® #8
Escape from Black Bear Mountain

Justin & Gary VanRiper
Copyright © 2008. All rights reserved.

First Paperback Edition, March 2008
Second Paperback Printing, May 2011

Cover illustration by Susan Loeffler
Illustrated by Carol McCurn VanRiper

Photograph of Coyote
© 2008 by Eric Dresser – www.nbnp.com

Published by
Adirondack Kids Press, Ltd.
39 Second Street
Camden, New York 13316
www.adirondackkids.com

Printed in the United States of America
by Patterson Printing, Michigan

ISBN 978-0-9707044-8-1

For Yogi & Nancy Best

Friends and supporters from day one

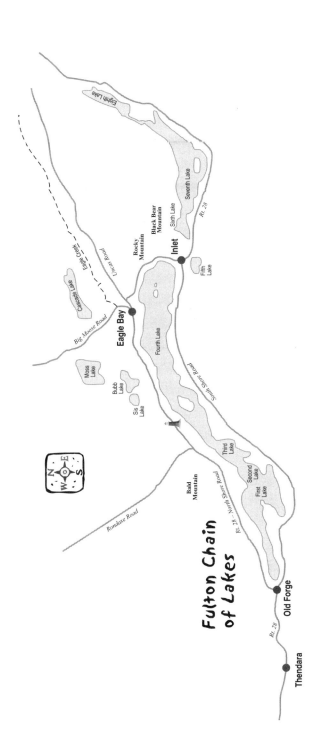

Fulton Chain of Lakes

Contents

"Do you see that?" Nick said.
"I told you, there is no way I am going
anywhere near those creepy monkeys."

1

Green with Envy

Justin Robert stood in the shadow of the towering lion and carefully aimed to get his best shot.

"Don't miss!" said his friend, Jackie Salsberry. "This may be your last chance!"

His friend, Nick Barnes, didn't offer much encouragement. "He'll choke," he said. "And it will be all over."

"No sweat," said Justin. He spoke boldly and with great confidence, but his palms were sweating, and the longer he waited to take the shot, the faster his heart pounded.

"Do it," said Nick. "Do it now."

Justin held his breath and softly tapped the purple ball. It rolled slowly through the lion's shadow, then through a tunnel, and emerged to hit a pinecone that had dropped into the middle of the green. Then the ball bounced gently off the brick wall and dropped straight into the center of the small silver cup.

"You did it!" said Jackie.

"Of course," said Justin.

"That was all luck," said Nick. The color of his

2

face matched his golf ball – dark red. "And I call interference. That pinecone was in the way."

Justin beamed. "I win – again," he said, as he plucked his purple ball from the hole. "So I get to choose what we do this afternoon – again." Then he tipped his silver bucket hat and bowed in the direction of the statue of the Tin Man. "Thank you, thank you," he said.

Jackie turned to Nick who was still brooding over Justin's third consecutive first-place finish that summer. "You would have a good chance to win if you would stop skipping the seventh hole," she said. "That costs you four penalty strokes every time we play."

Nick frowned and marched over to a sign that read: **Beware! Flying Monkeys**. Jackie and Justin followed him.

"Do you see that?" Nick said, and with great passion pointed his finger at the sign. Then he motioned the handle of his putter toward the treetops over the seventh hole, stabbing it into the air for emphasis. "I told you, there is no way I am going anywhere near those creepy monkeys. I didn't like them in the movie, and I don't like them here."

Justin held his bucket hat to his head, and ran back across the short path of yellow bricks. He struck a pose on the putting green, mimicking the large statue of the Cowardly Lion. "You should stand right here like this all day and take his place," he said, and laughed. "You need some courage."

"I do not," insisted Nick. He pointed at the Lion

3

and the Tin Man. "We only play golf here so Jackie can hang around these characters she likes so much from her favorite baby book, *The Wizard of Oz*."

"Have you ever read, *The Wizard of Oz*?" asked Jackie.

"I don't have to," said Nick. "I've only seen the movie with my parents, like, ten thousand times. They make me watch it." He glanced up at the tree-tops again suspiciously and with narrowed eyes. "I only skip the part with the monkeys."

Jackie sighed. "Then you don't know what you're talking about," she said. "The book is way different from the movie."

Justin nodded. "She's right," he said. "I was surprised. I read most of it, and it has some pretty gross stuff in it."

Nick suddenly seemed interested. "It does?" he said. "Can I borrow it?"

The thick evergreen branches above the seventh hole started shaking.

Justin and Jackie looked to see what was making the commotion so high up in the trees.

Nick didn't wait. As soon as he saw a branch begin to move, he started running for the parking lot as fast as his legs would carry him. He never saw the four black crows emerge from the canopy and fly off toward the highway.

Jackie turned to Justin and shook her head. "It's funny how your imagination can fool you, isn't it?" she said.

Justin nodded, but his mind was already on something else. He knew what he wanted to do with the rest of the day, but time was running short. "Let's go rescue Nick," he said, and they ran to join their friend in surrendering their golf balls and putters at the concession stand.

"It was only a bunch of crows," Jackie announced to their timid friend. She leaned against the counter and opened the scoring card to double-check the final totals.

"You don't have to do that," Nick said, and reached out to shake Justin's hand for winning. "So what are we doing this afternoon?" he asked, and hoped it would be fishing.

"Yes," said Jackie. "What's the plan?" She didn't care what they did, as long as it was something outside.

Justin's mom pulled into the parking lot in the family jeep. "You'll see," he said, as they piled into the vehicle for the brief ride back to Eagle Bay. "I'll tell you as soon as we get to camp."

Chapter Two

Warning Signs

"We'll take the yellow trail to the blue trail," said Justin. "We don't have much time and it's a lot shorter."

"I can't believe you picked hiking again," said Nick. "You knew I wanted to go fishing. Why didn't you pick fishing?"

Jackie never needed to be talked into hiking. The Adirondack native spent most of her free time all year somewhere in the woods with hiking boots on in the summer and snowshoes in the winter. "Be quiet, Nick," she said. "Justin won the game, so he gets to choose. And I think it is great he wants to climb every local mountain at least once before vacation is over."

Nick adjusted his small daypack and moaned.

Ever since Justin had overcome his fear of heights at the beginning of the summer on Bald Mountain, and after his adventure in the high peaks wilderness with his friends and grandfather on Algonquin Peak, he was eager to hike and climb. Located just across the highway from their camp property, the short ascent up Rocky Mountain just a week earlier had been easy, and now it was time for Black Bear. He also hoped to be the first ten-year-old to climb every local mountain – with a cat.

Justin stood on his tiptoes and swung open the door on the trail register to sign in their hiking party of three – actually, four, counting his calico side-kick, Dax. She was sitting patiently and grooming one of her back legs, the one with the tiger stripes.

"Hey, where did the register book go?" Justin said, feeling around with his hand. "The whole box is empty."

"Maybe someone took it for a souvenir," offered Nick.

Jackie looked perplexed. "This is really odd," she said. "There were quite a few cars in the parking lot. It's hard to believe that everyone is climbing Rocky."

Justin shrugged. "How would we know where anyone went without the book?" he said. "And, if everybody is climbing Rocky, then we'll have the whole top of Black Bear to ourselves."

"I'll just run over and check out the book at the Rocky trailhead," said Jackie. "Then we'll know for sure."

"No," Justin pleaded. "We don't have enough time. We have to go now."

"I don't know … " said Jackie.

"That's a maybe," said Justin, as he shut and locked the register door. "And a maybe is yes."

Before Jackie could further protest, he and Dax were

7

headed up the trail. Nick resigned himself to follow.

Jackie called out after them. "I don't think this is a good idea."

The stubborn trio kept walking, and she called out again. "I have all the water!" She held up a plastic bottle and waved it.

Nick stopped and looked back at her. "That's okay," he said, and cracked a sinister smile. He reached into his pocket, pulled out a granola bar and waved back at her. "I've got all the food!" Then he turned and hustled along to keep up with the leaders.

Jackie murmured in frustration. "Why do they always do this to me?" she said. Tucking the water bottle into a side pocket on her daypack, she ran to join them.

Not one of the young hikers noticed the small plywood sign at the trailhead, which had fallen face down on the ground. Now stained with muddy boot and paw prints, the plywood sign involuntarily hid its words of warning – **Trail Closed**.

Chapter Three

Making Tracks

As the three Adirondack kids steadily marched single file through the hardwood forest, the only sounds were the mud sucking at their boots and an occasional trickle of water that came from a small stream off to their left that ran along the Black Bear trail. Dax kept weaving from one side of the trail to the other, slowing down and speeding up, making the footing extra tricky for the hikers who were afraid they might step on her.

"Watch it, Dax," said Nick, who skipped to miss the cat and stubbed his boot on a rock instead. He stumbled forward and lost his valiant fight for balance when his other boot slid down into a narrow, shallow trench that was still slick from recent summer rain. He went sprawling nearly spread-eagle to the ground.

"Where did *that* come from?" asked Jackie.

Nick slowly rose to his feet. "I didn't do it on purpose," he said. "Dax made me fall."

"No," said Jackie. "I mean this." She swung both of her arms to trace two long, narrow impressions that ran side by side the length of the trail as far as they could see.

"Tire tracks?" said Justin. "Someone must have driven a car in here." He turned. "Look, they've been here all along. There are fewer rocks and stones and the ground is softer here, so the tracks are clearer."

Jackie shook her head. "But who would get permission to drive in here?" she said.

The sound of the stream suddenly had some competition. A low buzzing noise reached them from somewhere out in the woods.

"Black flies?" said Nick. He began itching his arms at the very thought of them.

"Not this time of year, silly," said Jackie.

"What about a chain saw?" Nick said, trying quickly to redeem himself.

Justin nodded. "It does sound like a chain saw," he said. "Maybe someone is doing some trail work – cutting up a fallen tree or broken branches."

Jackie wasn't convinced. "Something isn't right," she said. "And the way sound travels in the woods, whatever is making that noise could be miles from here. Let's keep going."

"I'm not going miles," said Nick.

Jackie stared him into walking.

"I'm just saying," said Nick, as he limped forward, "I'm not going miles. Just to the top of the mountain. That's it."

The buzzing sound grew louder as they finally approached the base of the mountain and entered the small clearing where the yellow trail broke left and the blue trail turned right.

"Well, we may not know what is making the buzzing noise yet," said Justin, as he and Dax stepped into the open space. "But at least we know what made the tracks."

"It's a – ," said Nick, and paused. "Actually, I'm not sure what it is."

"I don't really know what it is either," admitted Justin. "I've never seen anything like it."

"Oh, come on," said Jackie. "Haven't you boys ever gone to an antique car show? It's an old pick-up truck, probably 100 years old, with a special wooden box built onto the back to carry passengers."

The rear door of the old-fashioned station wagon was wide open. Dax approached the vehicle cautiously at first, and then leaped in to take a look around. Two sets of long, padded seats faced each other in the back of the vehicle. She sniffed the tarp that lay on the floor and then jumped onto one of the seats to peer out the window.

"How can it be that old?" said Nick. "The paint and the wood and all the silver parts are so shiny. It looks brand new."

They slowly circled the largely wood-paneled vehicle, admiring its unique shape with its narrow windshield and wide, black fenders. The four white-wall tires were stained mostly brown from its recent off-road travel, but a fifth tire mounted high on the side looked as white as new snow.

The rear door of the old-fashioned station wagon was open. Dax cautiously approached the vehicle.

"Some people collect old cars and trucks like this and fix them up," said Jackie. "This one is really quite fancy."

"Hey, it's staring at me," said Nick. Sure enough, facing the wagon from the front, the headlights looked like two bulging eyes, a portion of the grill a nose, with the bumper providing the suggestion of a long, narrow mouth. "Actually, it would make a great clubhouse," he said, making bug eyes back at the manmade creature. "When we get older, we could drive it around and have meetings anywhere."

"But what is it doing here, in the middle of the woods, on a wilderness trail?" wondered Justin, aloud.

"That's the big question," said Jackie.

"Hey, listen," said Nick. "The buzzing stopped."

Nick was right. The woods had once again gone silent.

That just made it easier to hear – the scream.

Chapter Four

Terror on the Trail

The three Adirondack kids stood with wide eyes, looking back and forth at one another.

Justin's goose bumps slowly faded and he finally blurted what all of them were thinking. "Was that a *person*?"

Nick was in denial. "No way," he said. "I am sure that was a bird."

His two friends looked at him.

"A really big bird," Nick continued, stretching his arms wide. "You know, like a giant eagle."

Jackie shook her head. "Are you serious?"

Justin couldn't help it. "Maybe it *was* Big Bird," he teased. "Like on Sesame Street."

"I didn't know you still watched that show," Nick shot back.

There was suddenly a second scream, and all humor and any doubt were erased. Because this time they all clearly heard the word – "Help!"

"Someone is definitely in trouble," said Jackie. "Maybe somebody was hurt using a chain saw, or a tree landed on him." She knew how to perform first aid, and without hesitation moved quickly up the herd path past the first blue trail marker, into the direction of the shrill and desperate cry.

Now it was Jackie in the lead and Justin and Nick in tow. Dax seemed content continuing to explore the inside of the wagon in the woods.

The blue trail up Black Bear Mountain was shorter than the yellow trail, but much steeper. Justin and Nick struggled to keep pace with Jackie, who seemed to glide up the winding, rocky pathway and momentarily disappear at nearly every turn.

"Slow down," pleaded Nick, who would have dropped his pack if it weren't loaded with snacks and lunch. Then he bumped into Justin, who had bumped into Jackie, who had stopped at a bend in the trail at the sound of several voices revealing a disturbing conversation.

"We've got you now, kid," they heard a man say.

"There's no one to help you way out here," said another. *"Just give yourself up."*

"Who is it?" whispered Nick. "Can you see?"

Jackie waved her hand, motioning for silence.

Justin turned and glared at him, raising his index finger to his lips. "Quiet," he said, silently mouthing the word.

They listened as a younger voice – a boy's voice – responded to the threats.

15

They managed to move just enough to allow
an orange motorcycle driven by a young boy to
skid by them, and peel off down the trail.

"All right, you've got me," the boy said. *"I give up."*

Justin, Jackie and Nick didn't know what to do. They did not have to know. The buzzing sound suddenly began again and was quickly headed their way.

It was useless to run. They managed to move just enough to allow a sleek, orange motorcycle driven by a young boy to come around the bend, skid by them, and peel off down the trail.

By the expression on the rider's face as he zoomed by, he was just as surprised to see them as they were to see him.

"Hey, get back here!" It was one of the angry men, now in hot pursuit of the escaping boy.

"We've got to find him," said the other. *"He knows too much."*

The voices of the two men were moving closer, and it was obvious to the three stunned friends what they should do.

"Run!" Jackie whispered, with urgency in her voice.

Her encouragement was not needed. Justin and Nick were already racing down the trail.

Chapter Five

Under Wraps

"Drop your packs," cried Justin, who flung his own pack while he ran. "You'll be able to run faster!"

Nick and Jackie never broke their stride as they dropped their packs along the side of the trail. It worked. With bodies barely under control, the three friends descended the trail in record time, sprinting out into the clearing. Their palms and arms were scratched from the pine tree trunks they had grabbed hold of on the way down in an effort to remain on the trail and manage their reckless descent.

"There's the motorcycle," said Justin, still panting. The orange machine rested against a small tree near the station wagon.

"But where's the boy?" asked Nick. He was bent over, his hands on his knees as he gulped for air. There was no sign of the wild, trail rider anywhere.

The men's voices had stopped, but they heard a branch snap from somewhere up the trail and knew someone was still on the chase.

"We've got to hide," continued Nick. "But I can't run any more."

"In here," said Justin, as he ran for the open back of the wagon. "We'll get under the tarp."

"Not a good idea," said Jackie. Her warning went unheeded, and within seconds the three friends were huddled together underneath the bulky cloth covering that lay in a heap on the floor of the classic vehicle.

Nick's voice squeaked. "I hear voices," he said. He closed his eyes and buried his head in his hands.

Jackie nudged Justin and whispered. "Where's Dax?"

Justin had forgotten all about her. He poked his head out from under the tarp and discovered her standing on the driver's seat. She was peering over the steering wheel for a glimpse out of the windshield. "Dax," he whispered. "Get down here!"

Dax continued to stand upright on the seat, sliding her front paws back and forth on the wheel as if she was steering the old wagon down a highway for a lazy summer drive.

The men's voices were calmer now, and very clear. One voice was high-pitched and raspy, as from a scratchy throat. The other voice was deep and booming, every word sounding like a beat on a large bass drum.

"Where do you think he went?" asked the raspy-throated man.

"Who knows?" boomed the other. *"He could be back to the highway by now."*

Dax was sliding her front paws back and forth
on the wheel as if she was steering the old
wagon down a highway for a lazy summer drive.

Justin called out to his calico sidekick again. "Dax," he said. "I mean it, get down here."

The men's disturbing conversation continued as they walked across the clearing and approached the wagon.

"Not without his motorcycle," the raspy-voiced man said, and laughed. *"Let's stick it in the back of the wagon."*

It was now or never. Justin took a chance. He slipped out from under the tarp, scooped Dax from the driver's seat with his left arm and slid back with her onto the floor and under cover again, just as one of the men approached the rear of the vehicle.

"No, wait." Again, the words boomed. *"Leave the cycle here. The others may still need it. I think I know where he went."*

"Others?" whispered Jackie. "There are more than two of them?"

"Hey, look at this," said the raspy-throated man. *"Muddy animal footprints are all over the back seats. Disgusting! I'll use the tarp to clean it up."*

The wagon bounced as the man grabbed the back door to hoist himself up.

Nick and Jackie held their breath and cringed. Justin held Dax closer.

21

"Let it be," said his partner. *"The prints are probably from that pesky raccoon. We'll let the kid clean it up when we find him. Let's go."*

With that, the man backed off and slammed the rear door of the wagon shut.

"Yes," whispered Nick. "They're finally leaving."

Sweet relief! Justin could not remember a time in his life when his stomach had felt so tight that it ached, except when he climbed the fire tower for the first time at Bald Mountain. He had survived that nightmare, and it looked like he would survive this nightmare as well. He felt his stomach muscles begin to relax – until the two front doors of the wagon opened and slammed shut.

The wagon shook under the combined weight of the two men as they entered the vehicle. Springs squeaked as they shifted in their seats to settle in for the ride.

"Shouldn't we at least throw the motorcycle into the back?" asked the raspy-throated man.

Justin could not imagine keeping quiet with the two tires of that heavy machine rolling over their backs. In fact, he figured it would probably squash them!

"No, I want to pick up the kid," boomed the driver. The temperature was blistering, and he rolled his window down to circulate the air. *"That boy sure*

22

has a lot of energy. He wants to go on foot? We'll take the easy way." A key turned and the old engine erupted into life. *"Let's get him."*

Justin and Jackie could hear Nick softly whisper from somewhere beneath the tarp. "We're doomed."

Chapter Six

Odd Behavior

It was a good thing the old engine was loud. The kids tried not to make a move or a sound, but it was hard to remain totally quiet and still. The vehicle continued to rock as it motored slowly down the bumpy, muddy trail. Even the men grunted when a tire would hit a large rock or drop into a hole, causing both of them to bounce around in their seats.

Dax loved hiding in dark, confined spaces, but not Justin. He whispered to his friends. "I can't breathe."

Before Jackie or Nick could stop him, he quickly poked his head out from under the tarp for a gasp of fresh air. He was disappointed as the air near the floor was not only warm, but thick with the fumes from gasoline. He took the opportunity to look up and caught a glimpse of the back of the driver's head and shoulders. He was wearing a large brown hat. It was the kind of hat he imagined hunters would wear while on a wildlife safari. A wide man with a thick neck, he also wore a tan vest over a red shirt and seemed to be sweating even more than he and his suffocating friends were underneath the heavy cloth. As the vehicle turned onto the highway, he felt a rapid tug on his pants from either Jackie or Nick – he couldn't tell which one – and quickly pulled his head back in under the tarp like a turtle into its shell.

Nobody said another word. Not the kids. Not the men. Not even when the wagon stopped and the passenger door opened and shut and then the wagon continued on again. All sense of time was lost when the vehicle finally turned again, and then again, before coming to an abrupt stop.

The engine ceased rumbling and both doors opened and closed.

The Adirondack kids still would not speak or budge. They did not dare. It took Dax to make the first move. She slipped from Justin's grasp and ran out from beneath the tarp and into the open, which gave him and his friends the courage to follow. Dripping with sweat, they kicked the tarp away and cautiously climbed onto a seat to peer out a window. What they saw they could not believe.

"We're in the Inlet parking lot?" Nick whispered. "We haven't gone far at all."

They scanned the parking lot for any sign of danger.

The resort hamlet was alive with activity. There were people moving in every direction, up and down the sidewalks. Others were crossing the busy highway that was lined with parked cars that carried campers and tourists who were shopping or going to a movie or a restaurant or waiting their turn at the *Northern Lights* for ice cream.

"It seemed like we were driving forever," Justin said, softly.

"You can stop whispering," said Jackie, who seemed more angry now, than frightened. "Those guys are gone. And they wouldn't dare do anything with all these people around."

Justin's head jerked forward and he pressed his index finger against the window pane. "That's him!" he said. He pushed open the wagon's back door and jumped out into the parking lot.

"That's who?" said Nick, who had his full attention focused on the ice cream shop. He and Jackie jumped out to join their animated friend on the pavement.

"The man that was driving," said Justin. He pointed toward the hamlet square. "It's the tall man with the brown hat. He's sitting over there on the bench."

"There's a boy sitting with him," said Jackie. "Where did *he* come from?"

"He's got ice cream," said Nick, and licked his parched lips.

"We've got to catch them," Justin said. "It might be the boy who was being chased on the motorcycle. That man will have to let him go in front of all these people."

"I'm really hot and could sure use some ice cream," said Nick.

"What about Dax?" asked Jackie, and picked the calico up before she could wander into the busy parking lot.

Justin turned to Nick. "Can you please take Dax to the *Adirondack Reader* and wait for us?"

"But Reggie doesn't have any ice cream there," Nick said.

"Come on, Nick," said Justin. "She has air-conditioning."

"And cold drinks," added Jackie.

Nick looked over at the book shop. "I don't know …" he said.

"You know what that means," Jackie said, and handed Dax over to him. "That's a maybe."

Justin finished. "And a maybe means yes."

The two took off in the direction of the boy and the man with the big brown hat. A bewildered Nick was left standing at the rear of the wagon with the cat in his arms.

Jackie called back to him. "Get going," she said. "Hey, see if the *Reader* has a copy of the *Wizard of Oz.*"

Chapter Seven

The Vanishing Boy

"Where did they go?" asked Justin. He and Jackie stood by the bench in the square. "They were here just a minute ago."

"There they are," said Jackie. "Up by the post office, near the library sign." She grabbed Justin's arm. "Let's go."

The man in the brown hat towered over the boy, who was still working on his ice cream cone. The two walked steadily up the sidewalk together, but did not appear in any hurry.

"Do you think it's the same boy we saw on the trail?" asked Justin, not sure how fast they should follow and with no real idea of what they would do if they actually caught up with them.

"I don't know," said Jackie. "That motorcycle went by so fast on the trail. And if it is the same boy, he's sure dressed all different now. Are you sure it's the same man?"

"Positive," said Justin, unconvincingly.

The boy and the man stopped at the crosswalk near the *Screamen' Eagle*. Traffic continued to be

28

heavy, both on the road and on the sidewalks.

Justin and Jackie also stopped a safe distance behind – or so they thought. As the boy pushed the tip of his cone into his mouth, he glanced over his shoulder and looked in their direction.

"Let's let him know he has friends," said Justin. Before Jackie could stop him, he smiled and waved.

Instead of returning a wave or a smile, the boy stopped chewing and broke into a run. Tires squealed as he darted across South Shore Road. The car stopped just in time to let him safely pass. Then the boy jumped onto the porch of the *Eagle* and into the front screen door. The man in the brown hat acted confused and hurried after him.

Justin's smile disappeared and he dropped his waving arm. "What is going on?" he thought out loud.

"I think he dropped something," said Jackie. "Come on."

In less than a minute they were inside the *Eagle* with a pair of lost sunglasses.

"Let's check the movie section first," suggested Justin, and the search for the boy began in several rooms where multiple rows of shelves held boxes of film titles for rent.

Jackie picked a box from a shelf. "Hey, here's the *Return to Oz,*" she said. "I haven't actually ever seen this one." She placed it back and continued to look over the other titles.

Justin didn't hear her. He was sticking to their mission. "The boy's not anywhere in the movie section,"

The boy glanced over his shoulder
and looked in their direction.

he called out. "I'm going to check at the counter. Are you coming?"

It was hard to stand in front of the many fresh-baked pies while they waited for the girl at the register to serve her long line of paying customers – some holding movie rentals and some to pick up their orders for take-out.

Justin stared at the pies that lined the counter and drooled. "It's a good thing Nick isn't here," he said.

A woman with her hair gathered into a net emerged from the kitchen, wiping her hands on a towel. "Can I help you?" she said.

"Yes," said Jackie. "We are looking for a boy who dropped these sunglasses on the street." Justin held them up for the lady to see. "We were sure the boy came in here."

"Yes," said Justin. "He was with a large man who had a big brown hat on. It was the kind of hat like people wear when they hunt for lions."

"Let me check with the girls," the woman said.

Justin shoved the sunglasses into his pocket for safe keeping. He and Jackie watched as the lady from the kitchen spoke with the girl at the counter.

"Why are they whispering?" said Justin.

"Shhh, here she comes," said Jackie.

"I am so sorry," the lady said. "We haven't noticed anyone come in here today that fits that description." Then she pointed at the tables filled with customers who were in the dining area behind them. "But it is possible we could have missed them with so many people in and out of here today."

Justin started to ask another question, but Jackie interrupted as she took hold of his arm. "We understand," she said. "Thank you, anyway."

"Why did you make me stop talking?" asked Justin as they exited the *Eagle* and started back up the sidewalk to join Nick and Dax at the book shop.

"Think about it," said Jackie. "We don't even know if that was the same boy that was in trouble. And we don't have any idea what the other man in the wagon looked like. He could be anywhere around here and we wouldn't even know it."

That made Justin nervous, and he began to look at every stranger on the sidewalk with suspicion. He plucked the sunglasses from his pocket and put them on.

"What are you doing?" asked Jackie.

"Wearing a disguise," said Justin. "So no one will know who I am."

Jackie shook her head. "We need to be serious, Justin," she said. "This isn't a movie – this is real."

"You're right," said Justin. "We should walk back to camp right now and tell our parents, or Ranger Bill. They'll know what to do." He was actually relieved they weren't going to try to handle the situation alone. And after sweating under a dirty tarp and now having to walk the mile back to camp from Inlet, a jump in the cool waters of Fourth Lake seemed like a great idea.

"Good," said Jackie. "I'm glad we finally agree on something."

The *Adirondack Reader* was ahead, just beyond the parking lot. They could see Nick holding Dax, pacing back and forth on the book shop's front porch.

"I just want to check one thing before we meet up with Nick," Justin said.

Jackie sighed. "What now?"

"The license plate on the old wagon," Justin said. "If we write down the letters and numbers, that might help mom and dad when they check things out." He dashed into the parking lot to get a quick look.

"We don't even have a pen or anything to write on," protested Jackie. She followed him even though she was not happy with the sudden detour.

It didn't matter.

A bewildered Justin stood at the trunk of a small, blue sedan that had two kayaks mounted on top. "I know the wagon was parked right here," he said, and turned to Jackie. "It's already gone!"

Chapter Eight

Stranded

Justin and Jackie sat stunned on *the Rock* at their secret meeting place. It was Pioneer Village – that small community the Adirondack kids built of sticks every summer in the woods between Justin's and Nick's family camps – where no adults were allowed.

Nick simply crossed his legs and yawned. "Well, did you tell them everything?" he said.

Justin was defensive. "Yes," he said. "I told mom and dad every single thing – about the wagon and the men and the boy yelling for help – everything. It's like they didn't believe anything I told them – like I was exaggerating."

"I told my mom and dad everything, too," said Jackie, obviously greatly annoyed at their indifference. She gestured toward Justin. "I know my parents called and talked to your parents. And I thought for sure they would call Ranger Bill, at least about the trail being torn to pieces by a motorcycle."

Nick shrugged. "I figured your parents would do something, so I didn't tell my mom and dad anything.

Justin and Jackie looked at him as if he was a traitor.

"What?" Nick said, trying to ignore their icy stares. "So, I just went swimming and right to reading, *The Wizard of Oz*."

That redirected Jackie. She acted shocked. "So Reggie found you a copy yesterday at the *Reader*?" she asked.

"I forgot to ask," Nick said. "My mom had a real old copy in the cabinet by the fireplace. The pages are all turned brown and it smells funny. It made me sneeze when I opened it." He felt an itch and rubbed his nose. It was as if the very thought of that smell might make him sneeze again. "I never even knew the book was there."

Jackie folded her arms across her chest. "And you're actually going to *read* it?"

Nick frowned. "No, I'm going to eat it," he said. "Yes, I'm going to read it." He paused. "At least until I find the gross part you and Justin were talking about."

There was a low rumble of thunder as Justin laid back on *the Rock* and stared up through the tangle of branches at the darkening sky. "I don't get it," he said. "My parents didn't even seem bothered. While I was talking, they just kept smiling. And today they want to treat us with another trip to Old Forge and a movie at the Strand."

"It sounds good to me," said Nick. "It's supposed to rain all day long. I vote we go."

There was another rumble of thunder, and then

the first bulging drop of rain made its way through the forest canopy and splashed upon *the Rock.*

Justin and Jackie looked at each other and shrugged. "Might as well," Justin said. Jackie agreed.

The smell of melted butter saturated the air. Justin loved the Strand. There were a lot of good reasons for it. He liked looking at the dozens of odd cameras that were on display everywhere throughout the historic theatre.

And every year he would check out the box of rolled-up movie posters in the lobby and use some of his allowance to buy an authentic poster from his favorite movie of the summer. His personal poster collection plastered his bedroom wall at his home back in Camden. He hadn't chosen this season's poster yet. There were still two more weeks before Labor Day.

But the thing he loved most about the Strand was going with his dad to the special midnight showings of the newly-released films. "See you guys in the morning," his mom would always say, when they left camp after a late supper. And usually theirs would be the only car on the road at 2 a.m., winding along Route 28 in the pitch black, returning from Old Forge to Eagle Bay. He and his dad would use the time to relive every action scene they could remember from the movie.

"Hey, Justin, are you going to buy a ticket today, or not?" asked Nick. It was more the sudden shove than his friend's voice that snapped Justin back from his daydream. "The matinee is going to start in five minutes, and we don't even have our popcorn yet."

The three friends selected their favorite treats and hurried through the large swinging doors that led them into the main auditorium.

"We are not sitting in the front row," said Jackie, already warning Nick who was quickly shuffling ahead with his large popcorn and soda.

"Fine," Nick said, and stopped about two-thirds of the way down the center aisle. "I still get the end seat." He waited as Justin and Jackie took the inside chairs, and then sat down himself as the auditorium went dark. "We just made it," he said.

As the first movie trailer began to roll, there was the muted sound of thunder, and they knew another round of pounding rain was about to hit.

"Hey, you guys, I just thought of something," said Nick.

"Shhh," said Jackie. "Don't start talking already."

Nick tried again. "But …"

"Quiet," whispered Jackie, so forcefully, she might just as well have screamed it.

Shushes sounded from all around them, and Nick sank deep down into his purple padded seat.

Justin loved to watch all the previews of the upcoming films. Maybe there would be another movie he and his dad could catch at a midnight showing. As the movie trailers continued to roll, Nick took the opportunity to excuse himself and hurried to the bathroom.

The images of the third trailer flashed quickly across the silver screen. Imagination quickly displaced reality, and if there was any more thunder, the soundtrack booming from the speakers drowned out any hint of it.

Justin shifted forward in his seat, and dropped his peanut butter cup. "It's already coming out," he whispered, excitedly. "I can't believe it."

"It figures you would like something like this," whispered Jackie, who kept flinching from the flashes of light caused by a constant barrage of on-screen explosions.

"Well, I do," said Justin, his eyes riveted to the screen. "I've read every book in the collection and knew the movie was coming out." He folded his hands as if in prayer as he waited to hear the release date. "Please, let it be soon."

Jackie shook her head. "It's okay, I guess, if you like a junior James Bond dressed up in silly clothes and doing crazy stunts that are humanly impossible. But I like stories that could really happen."

Justin glanced at her. "You mean like your favorite book, *The Wizard of Oz*?"

"That story was all a dream," Jackie countered, defensively.

"Not according to the book," said Justin. He could not see her cheeks flush in the dark, but he could tell by the size of her eyes reflecting in the light from the screen that he had struck a nerve. "You didn't think I read enough of the book to know that, did you?"

38

Jackie quickly changed the subject by pointing to the screen. "Look," she said. "Your silly movie is coming out this Friday."

"Yes!" said Justin, who had all he could do not to cheer right out loud. He clenched his fists. "Midnight showing on Thursday night!"

"Since it's suddenly okay to talk now," said Nick, as he slipped back into his seat, "all I was trying to tell you guys before is that we forgot and left our packs out on the trail. And right now they are in the pouring rain getting ruined." Then he sat back in his seat, swallowed a mouthful of soda, and burped.

Chapter Nine

A No-Brainer

It was a simple plan. A no-brainer.

"We'll just grab our packs and get back out of the woods as quick as we can," said Justin, as he hit the kickstand on his bike. He removed Dax from the small basket near the handlebars and set her on the ground. "And then it's breakfast at the Tamarack," he added, for the benefit of a dejected Nick.

The stubborn summer storm had persisted throughout the day before and finally passed sometime during the night. The pre-dawn air was fresh and crisp. The leaves on the trees were moist and shiny and perfectly still, and would soon dry out in the easy breeze that would gradually join the slowly rising Adirondack sun.

Nick and Jackie rested their bicycles against the same large boulder in the trailhead parking lot near the Black Bear Mountain sign.

"I know my pack is ruined," Nick said. "And even if it isn't, I'm sure some chipmunks or squirrels got in it and stole all the food."

Justin was the first one to notice the propped-up

40

sign as they approached the register. "The trail is closed?" he said. "What's going on?"

Nick shrugged, obviously not unhappy. "Oh, well, we might as well go get our breakfast now," he said, already headed back for his bike. "I'm going to have three pieces of French toast, one egg over easy, and some grapefruit juice. What are you guys having?"

"No," said Jackie. "We'll stick to the plan. All we're going to do is find our packs and leave."

"But what if there is something really wrong?" said Nick. "Maybe the stream is all flooded. I don't even have socks on."

"Good," said Jackie. "Then you won't have to dry them out."

Nick persisted. "But what if that weird wagon is there again, and those mean men?"

"Then you can hitch a ride and keep your feet dry," Jackie shot back.

Justin started up the trail. "Come on, you guys," he said. "We could have already been there and back to order our breakfast by now."

Nick groaned in frustration. "I can taste it already," he said, and then an insect flew into his open mouth. He began coughing uncontrollably, bent over and started to gag.

Jackie began to tap him on his back. "Need some water, Nick?" she asked.

Nick couldn't stop coughing. He tried to stand up straight, and with a hand cupped over his mouth, nodded his head up and down.

"Fine," Jackie said. She had no mercy. "There's water in my pack. Let's go!"

This time as they hiked, the kids kept their eyes focused on the ground. After their scary ride two days earlier, it was hard not to look for any signs of fresh wagon tracks.

"Here are some different ones," said Nick, his eyes still watering from his coughing spell. He stuck his boot into the broad, muddy valley. "They must be new. They're a lot bigger than the last ones we saw."

Jackie shook her head. "No," she said. "They're probably the same tracks from two days ago – just eroded and spread out by all that rain."

The boys nodded and they trekked on. The confidence in Jackie's voice, especially in times of doubt, was always reassuring. And she was almost always right when it came to interpreting signs in the wilderness.

Without the weight of their packs to slow them down, and motivated by a touch of anxiety, they made great time to the clearing at the base of the mountain.

"Not again," said Nick.

Justin looked at Jackie for confirmation. "It's a flatbed truck, right?" he said.

Nick was puzzled. "You mean people sleep on it?"

Jackie placed her hands on her hips. "This is ridiculous," she said. "This flatbed is even wider than the wagon was."

"So I guess I was right about the tracks," said Nick. "They were new, right?"

Jackie sighed. "Yes, you were right, Nick."

"And I guess that means you were wrong, right?" said Nick, smiling.

"Yes," said Jackie, refusing to let him upset her. "For the first and only time this entire summer, you were finally right."

Nick stopped smiling.

"Come on, you guys," said Justin, adjusting the placement of his boots, which were slowly beginning to sink in the oozing mud. Dax sat at his feet, her posture revealing the white fur down her neck and belly were now as dark as the patches of brown and black on her side and her back. "Forget about the truck," he said. "Let's find our packs and get to Inlet."

It didn't take long to reach the point in the trail where they had been nearly run over by the motorcycle and then chased off the mountain by the two men.

Jackie abruptly stopped. "We've already gone too far," she said. "We never reached this giant birch with the blue trail marker on it. Let's go back down slowly. Our packs have to be somewhere near here, right along the edges of the path.

With the vegetation still thick and high along both sides of the trail, the search was difficult, making the hike back down painstakingly slow.

"Our stuff could be two feet away and we would never see it," said Justin, as he pushed aside entire branches heavy with leaves to get clear views of the ground. He turned to Jackie. "You might have to come back and find everything for us after summer vacation in the fall when all the leaves are gone."

Nick was quite discouraged. "Unless someone else has already found everything and took it," he said.

Jackie waited patiently until the two boys had finished complaining and pointed toward the sky. "Well, no one took Justin's pack," she said.

"You sure are a great tracker," said Nick. "We walked right underneath it two times and never noticed it was there."

"I didn't find it," said Jackie. "Dax did." The calico sat in the middle of the trail staring upward.

"How did it get way up there?" said Justin. His small, gray daypack was suspended like a hornets' nest on a large branch high over their heads.

Jackie shook her head. "I don't know," she said. "You're the one who told us to drop our packs when we were running." She helped Justin shimmy up the thin trunk of a nearby tree so he could reach over and shake his daypack free. "I didn't hear you say to whip them as high as we could into the air."

"Look out, Dax," said Justin. The pack finally fell to the ground with a loud *thump*.

Since Justin had launched his pack when he gave everyone else the command to drop them, Jackie figured her pack couldn't be far away. It wasn't. "Got it," she said with satisfaction, holding it above her head with both arms like a championship trophy received at an award ceremony.

"Uh-oh," said Nick, who was poking around

44

"How did it get way up there?" said Justin.
His gray daypack was suspended like a hornets'
nest in the branches high over their heads.

45

some bushes on the opposite side of the trail.

"What's wrong?" asked Justin.

Nick held up part of a wrapper from a granola bar. And then another, and another. "This can't be good," he said, and stopped. The small paper trail led him to his greatest fear.

"Well, did you find it?" asked Justin.

Nick answered by lifting up and displaying his own pack that was now in a condition similar to the granola bar wrappers. He reached down to scoop up the rest of the litter, stashing the trash into his freshly shredded bag.

Jackie chuckled. "Mine has all the food in it," she mocked, doing the best impression of Nick's voice and body language she possibly could.

Justin's smile disappeared when he swung his pack over his shoulder. Still wet from the downpour, it felt clammy as it pressed against his back, soaking his T-shirt. "We got what we came for," he said. "Let's get out of here."

Nick groaned. "Not again," he said.

"What's wrong now?" asked Jackie.

Nick did not have to reply. This time they all heard it.

It was the distant sound of a motor – and another cry for help.

Chapter Ten

All Rise

"That's not a motorcycle this time," said Justin.

"And it's not a chain saw," said Nick.

"Helicopter," said Jackie. "That is absolutely a helicopter. And flying that low? Someone is definitely in trouble."

"Where are you going?" asked Nick, as Jackie pushed him aside and began moving quickly back up the blue trail.

Justin knew from the way she was marching it was useless to try and call her back. "We had better stay together," he said to Nick.

Three kids and a cat moved up the trail single file, the hikers on watch for the small blue discs marking the way, and ears alert for any more distress calls. The higher they climbed up the mountain, the fainter became the hum of the helicopter.

"We're near the summit now," said Jackie. As they pressed on, their boots passed over fewer roots and less mud, and more solid rock. "I know a short-cut from here," she said. "Follow me."

"Big noise!" "Big noise!" someone called out,

and a large bang and whooshing sound caused the three Adirondack kids to throw themselves to the ground. Justin watched helplessly as Dax disappeared into some bushes.

"What was *that?*" asked Nick, who bent his arm to check out a new scrape on his elbow.

"There's only one way to find out," said Jackie, and slowly she began crawling forward.

"Dax," whispered Justin. "Come here." To his surprise, Dax popped her head from among the bushes and then, as if nothing had happened, pranced out onto the stony surface to join him. He lifted his head to see Jackie inching her way toward the open summit. Then there was another bang, followed by the same whooshing sound, that this time took longer to stop.

Still creeping forward, Jackie turned her head and awkwardly motioned for Justin and Nick to stay low and keep moving toward her. The pain caused by the bumpy rockface against their bare palms and knees went unnoticed as their minds raced to identify the source of the mysterious sound. They gathered together into crouching positions behind a large boulder. Not one of them could muster the courage to peer out over the top of their hiding place.

"What if it's a bear?" said Nick.

Justin took off his bucket hat and used it to slap the arm of his friend. "If that's a bear, then why does it sound as big as Godzilla?" he said.

"Oh, great," said Nick. "That makes me feel a *lot* better."

Jackie reached into her pack.

"You have food and didn't tell me?" Nick was upset.

"Quiet," Jackie said, and pulled a small mirror from her first-aid kit.

"You're going to put some make-up on *now*?" asked Nick. "So, you want to look good for the monster before he eats us?"

Jackie sighed. He knew she didn't wear make-up. "I'm going to try and get a look around the rock with this," she said, and cradled the mirror in the palm of her hand. Holding it out just beyond the edge of the boulder, she carefully positioned it to reflect a view of the open summit.

"Do you see anything?" asked Justin. "What's out there?"

Jackie snapped the mirror shut and started to stand up.

"What are you doing?" said Justin. He grabbed at her shoulder in an attempt to stop her. He failed.

There was a short bang and a whoosh and a voice called out, "Don't worry, the police will come for you – if the coyotes don't get you first!"

Justin and Nick rose to join Jackie and together they watched as a boy wearing goggles and a red scarf waved and slowly floated into the sky.

Nick shook his head. "A hot air balloon? Up here?" He was amazed. They all were.

"Isn't that the same boy that was on the motor-cycle?" said Jackie.

Short bursts of burning fuel continued to feed hot

air into the balloon's massive envelope, blowing it up like a giant piece of bubble gum and carrying the basket with its young passenger higher and higher.

"If it is him, he's not going far with all those ropes hanging down," said Justin. "Look, one is stuck on a tree."

"Who is he waving at?" said Jackie. "I don't see anybody."

The sound of the balloon's burner was drowned out by an approaching helicopter.

"I knew that was a copter we heard before," said Justin. "It must be the police."

Together the three friends began to sprint across the long, flat summit, their packs bouncing against their backs. They stopped directly below the balloon, arms waving at the boy rising in the oval patchwork of blue, green and orange panels – the colorful envelope perfectly framed by a cloudless sky.

Another small head peered out over the edge of the basket.

"Who is with the boy?" said Nick.

"It's a raccoon!" said Justin.

Then another head appeared.

"How many people and animals are up there, anyway?" said Nick. "There's more of them than there are of us." Then he noticed Justin and Jackie had stopped waving. "What's wrong?" he asked.

"That's the man," Justin said.

"What man?" asked Nick.

They stopped directly below the balloon, arms
waving at the boy rising in the oval patchwork of
blue, green and orange panels – the colorful envelope perfectly framed by a cloudless sky.

51

Jackie frowned. "It's the man who drove the old station wagon."

"Hey, the balloon is stuck," said Justin. "It's not going up any more."

"It's actually coming back down," said Jackie.

Nick began to back away. "That balloon looks really old," he said. "We'd better move. If it pops, it might land right on us!"

As they slowly retreated, they heard growling from somewhere behind them. The bushes shook, and then there was a howl!

Chapter Eleven

Chaos on the Mountain

It was difficult to tell which was louder; Justin, Jackie and Nick yelling together, or the howling coyote that appeared from the bushes to stand on a large boulder directly in front of them.

So suddenly at eye level with the bare-fanged animal, the Adirondack kids went totally silent and were frozen in place. Then two more snarling coyotes slowly walked out onto the boulder to join their aggressive canine companion.

Justin felt his heart pounding. Without moving his head, he shifted his eyes back and forth quickly, looking for any sign of Dax. He saw her, also standing perfectly still, on the front fender of … the orange motorcycle? She was safe – for the moment.

"Maybe the balloon will scare them away," Jackie whispered, as a shadow, first cast from the basket, and then from the gigantic, swollen envelope, began to rest on their position. The shadow grew larger and darker, encircling them all, as the balloon dropped closer to the ground.

It didn't matter. Neither beast nor human moved.

The coyote appeared from the bushes to stand
on a large boulder directly in front of them.

It was a standoff.

And then there were voices everywhere. "Cut!" "Cut!" "Cut!" It was like an echo resounding all over the summit from every direction.

A woman appeared with a walkie-talkie in her hand. She was tall and had flame-red hair pulled back into a ponytail that swayed like a clock's pendulum as she marched.

The coyotes immediately sat down on the boulder, and one of them yawned.

"We're saved!" said Nick.

"Where did these kids come from?" the woman asked, her long legs carrying her quickly toward them. With cheeks aflame, nearly as red as her hair, she didn't sound happy.

"We're doomed," said Nick.

"Where did *we* come from?" said Jackie. "Where did *she* come from?"

"Who cares?" said Justin. He took advantage of the coyotes' sudden disinterest in them and bolted for Dax.

The balloon was almost on the ground and five more people appeared from behind trees and boulders, rushing to take hold of the suspended wicker basket to help ease it down onto the open rockface.

The woman with the ponytail barked some orders into the walkie-talkie. "Get the wranglers out here for the coyotes – secure the perimeter – reset, going again – and no more surprises, people."

A girl holding a clipboard ran up to join her. "I'm

55

so sorry, I have no idea how this happened. It seems these children just – "

"Not now," the woman with the ponytail said, and pointed the antennae of her walkie-talkie toward Justin who was sprinting across the summit. "Hey, where is that boy going?" She sighed and looked at the girl with the clipboard. "Go get him," she said, firmly. "And then bring all three of those kids to me."

Justin finally reached Dax. He tried to grab her, but she avoided his grasp. Jumping from the motor-cycle, the spry calico ran in the direction of the grounded balloon. As Justin ran after Dax, the girl with the clipboard ran after Justin.

There were people swarming the summit surface now, some even bumping into one another.

Nick sat down on the boulder next to the coyotes and pulled a surviving chunk of a granola bar from his torn pack. He turned toward the animal sitting closest to him. "Want some?" he asked, and quickly popped the small morsel into his own mouth. "I didn't think so," he said as he chewed.

Jackie simply shook her head, and turned to face the chaos continuing to unfold all around them on the mountain.

Chapter Twelve

Flying High

Justin, Jackie and Nick stood quietly side-by-side under a small stand of short trees. The girl with the clipboard stood silently with them, and was nervously tapping her foot.

It was still early morning, but Justin's slight shiver was not caused by the cooler temperature from standing in the shade. The prickly goose bumps on the back of his neck and running along his arms were caused by the conference of stern-looking adults gathered a few feet away from them. He had seen those looks on his parents' faces before, usually after he had done something terribly wrong.

Jackie was concentrating more on the strange-looking equipment that was scattered everywhere. Nick had his eye on a box of donuts sitting on a small fold-up chair.

Everyone was listening to the woman with the ponytail as she motioned toward the three Adirondack kids and then pointed out toward the grounded hot air balloon. "It's handled," they heard her say, mainly toward a woman with long dark hair in the middle of the group, who appeared to be the group's true leader. "We got the shot."

With that announcement, the girl with the clipboard stopped tapping her foot and sighed. All in the group notably relaxed, and Justin relaxed with them. He tightened just a little as the woman with the dark hair now turned her full attention upon them.

"We didn't do anything wrong," Justin blurted as she approached, and he quickly wondered where the sudden burst of courage had come from, to defend himself and his friends.

"Pardon me?" the woman said.

"We were just getting our packs," said Nick. "Look, mine is all ripped." He held up what was left of his shredded bag to show her. "I thought squirrels ruined it, but maybe it was them." He turned dramatically to point at the coyotes, but they were gone.

The woman looked puzzled. "So, you didn't see the sign that said the trail was closed?"

Nick caved. "That's what I told them," he said, gesturing nervously toward Justin and Jackie. "All I wanted to do was go to the Tamarack and get some French toast and eggs …"

Jackie came to their rescue. "We weren't planning on climbing to the top of the mountain at all," she said. "We were looking for our lost packs and it sounded like someone was in trouble and so we ran up here to help."

The woman didn't say anything, but Jackie never lost eye contact with her. "I know first aid," Jackie

58

said, firmly and without blinking.

The woman broke into a smile. "So, everything you heard and saw seemed quite real?"

The three friends nodded.

Justin glanced at all of the equipment and activity still going on behind her. "Are you making – a movie?" he asked.

"Yes, we are," the woman said. "My name is Joy, and I am a co-producer and the director.

"A real movie?" said Nick. "Can I be in it?"

Jackie blushed. "Maybe by accident we already are," she said.

"Listen," the director said, thoughtfully. "Can you keep quiet? Do you want to come and watch the last shot?"

They nodded again.

With that, she looked to the girl with the clipboard. "Take them to Owen and stay with them." Then quickly excusing herself, she hustled off toward the balloon.

"I'm Gayle," said the girl with the clipboard.

"Who was that tall woman with the ponytail who was bossing everyone around?" asked Nick.

Gayle smiled. "She's an assistant director," she said. "Her name is Sharon." They walked only a few feet where a man was kneeling down with a large camera on a tripod, everything slightly hidden among some bushes. "And this is Owen."

The cameraman waved, but his eyes never left the equipment in front of him, which also included a large monitor, filled at the moment with a close-up image of the boy and raccoon in the basket of the balloon. They all watched as several adults were fussing with the young actor's hat and goggles and scarf while Joy spoke to him. Another man was feeding something to the raccoon.

"Do you get any other channels?" asked Nick, and giggled.

Jackie frowned at him.

Justin studied the boy on the monitor. Seeing the actor's face in such detail, he looked familiar. As Justin thought about where he might have seen the boy before, he was distracted as the man from the station wagon suddenly appeared on the screen.

Nick pointed at the monitor and blurted out what Justin was hesitant to ask. "Who is that big guy with the funny hat?"

Jackie poked her elbow into Nick's side. "We were told to be quiet," she whispered, although she, too, was very curious to know the identity of the mystery man.

"That's okay," said Owen. "The guy with the hat? We were really lucky to find him. He owns and operates hot air balloons, including that beauty we are using here right now. It really is a modern balloon, but was designed to look like it's much older."

They all continued to watch the monitor as the man with the funny hat climbed into the basket and disappeared. "He sits down so the camera doesn't see him," Owen explained. "Then it looks like Mack is the one actually flying the balloon."

"Mack?" said Justin. It suddenly occurred to him where he might have seen the boy before. "Is that Mack Carson?"

"Yes, it is," said Gayle. "We were fortunate to get him, too. He and the balloon man have actually become great friends this past week."

"Who is Mack Carson?" asked Nick.

Justin could not stop staring at the monitor. "Mack Carson is in the movie I'm going to see at the Strand this weekend," he said. "I can't believe it's him."

"So that's who was with the balloon man in Inlet," said Jackie. "No wonder he was wearing sunglasses and running away from us in town."

Nick grinned. "What's the big deal about that?" he said. "If I didn't know you, I'd try to run away from you, too!"

The sound of the approaching helicopter filled the air again, and Joy returned to their hiding place in the trees to watch the monitor. The woman with the ponytail joined them. Everyone except the actors disappeared behind boulders and into the bushes and trees.

Joy took hold of the walkie-talkie. "Okay, folks – let's do this."

The helicopter with its own camera was upon them now and hovering over the summit.

Voices sounded again. "Rolling." "Rolling." "Rolling." The word echoed everywhere over the mountain.

Joy handed the walkie-talkie to the assistant director.

"Action, villains!" Sharon commanded, fire in her voice. "Action, balloon!"

As the burners fired, the weights and ropes holding the balloon in place dropped to the ground. Two actors dressed in old-fashioned clothing ran out onto the summit, shaking their fists up at the boy as he and his raccoon and the hidden balloon man in their basket slowly rose into the air.

"Dax!" said Justin.

They all saw her on the monitor at the same time, poking her head just above the basket's edge, very near to the acrobatic raccoon.

"Get the cat out of the shot," said the director, calmly.

Sharon nodded. She spoke into her walkie-talkie addressing the balloon man. "Have Mack hand the cat down to you," she said.

Everyone's eyes were fixed to the monitor; and after a long pause, the director broke the silence. "Got that," said Joy. "Very good."

"That's a cut for the crew," said Sharon. "Camera's still rolling on the balloon." She turned to Justin. "We have a chase crew following the balloon. Gayle will be sure your cat is returned to you."

Justin nodded, but was mesmerized by the balloon that was now floating far and away over the lush Adirondack landscape. He wondered what it would be like to see the trees and lakes and rivers and mountains from so high in the sky. *Someday I will be as brave as Dax and I'll see for myself,* he thought.

"Hey, that looked just like the balloon scene from the *Wizard of Oz*," said Nick. "Except like with Toto flying away." He turned to Jackie. "Isn't this when you click your boots together and say, 'there's no place like camp'?"

"No," said Jackie. "This is when I snap my fingers and say, 'pay no attention to that silly boy behind the bushes.'"

Chapter Thirteen

Midnight Showing

"Come here, Argus," said Justin. The Siberian Husky eagerly pranced into his waiting arms. Justin loved the feeling of the fur between his fingers when he buried his hands deep into the theatre mascot's thick coat. Argus really liked it, too.

"Keep him away from my popcorn," said Nick, who was now carefully studying the rows of candy neatly lined up inside the glass counter.

He was joined by a throng of equally hungry patrons who were scanning the blackboards that were positioned high on the wall behind the cashier, where snack selections and prices were neatly spelled out in neon-colored chalk.

Midnight showings of new films at the Strand Theatre in Old Forge were always a big hit with both the locals and the tourists – but tonight was huge. A brand new family movie based on a best-selling book would have been enough to draw a large crowd, but this movie also featured one of Hollywood's favorite childhood stars – Mack Carson. Rumors were even buzzing that Carson had been seen shopping, playing and eating at restaurants in the immediate area during the week. Some people were even saying an action movie was being filmed nearby, based on a book set in the Adirondacks.

"There's his name, right on top," said Justin to Jackie. They were standing in front of a colorful, action-filled piece of artwork in a giant gold frame that was mounted on a wall in the foyer. "There is no question which movie poster I am adding to my collection this summer. Mr. Card thinks he has an extra one he's going to give me tonight." He motioned to the theatre owner who was standing in sandals on a small ladder wearing a Hawaiian shirt and baggy jeans, leafing through posters hidden behind one of the other frames. Argus was looking up from the foot of the ladder, as if he was helping in the search.

Jackie couldn't stand it any longer. "Take those silly things off," she said, and reached for Justin's sunglasses.

Justin ducked and pulled away. "Stop," he said, and picked up his bucket hat, which had dropped to the carpet. "We should all be wearing a pair of these, so no one notices us."

Jackie tried to reason with him. "It is almost midnight," she said. "That means it is the – middle – of – the – night," she added for emphasis. "And you are wearing sunglasses."

"So?" Justin said.

Jackie sighed. "And you think no one is going to notice you?"

Mr. Card was standing on a small ladder and
leafing through posters hidden behind one of the
frames. Argus looked up from the foot of
the ladder, as if he was helping in the search.

66

"It doesn't matter, anyway," said Justin, and shrugged. "Everybody's paying attention to Argus."

It was true. No one could resist taking a lingering look at the beautiful and friendly animal, wagging his tail and spotting for his master.

Holding a large popcorn and soda, Nick finally joined his friends. "Do you think he's still coming?" he asked. A pack of strawberry licorice stuck out of his back pocket.

"Quiet," said Jackie, and whispered. "If people know he might be here, we'll never get to see him or the movie."

Justin glanced at his watch. He was disappointed. "The movie's going to start in a few minutes. I guess he's not going to make it."

Nick tried to talk while swallowing a handful of popcorn. "Balloon man," he managed to blurt out and pointed, before starting to cough.

"Then he's got to be here somewhere," said Justin, hopefully.

"Hi, guys," said a voice behind them.

The three friends turned around, and Justin was face-to-face with Mack Carson. Actually, he was hat-to-hat. A large and perfect smile was all anyone could see underneath the oversized bucket hat the actor was wearing to help disguise his identity.

"You made it!" Justin said.

The balloon man walked past them and winked as he flashed his ticket and pushed through the powder-blue doors into the main auditorium.

"Of course I made it," said Mack. "I heard this was a great movie."

Justin removed his sunglasses and handed them to the actor. "They're the ones you dropped in Inlet," he said.

Mr. Card approached and handed Justin a rolled-up poster. "There you go," he said. "You'd all better get inside – I saved you four seats near the front. The film is about to begin."

"Can't Argus sit with us?" asked Jackie. She reached down to pet him.

Nick held his popcorn close and looked at her like she was crazy.

"Not tonight," said Mr. Card, and smiled. "We've got a full house."

epilogue

Justin stretched out on his bed and stared up at the poster now hanging above his head on the ceiling of the sleeping porch.

The people making the movie had all left town, and word about the visiting actors and film crew was spreading like wildfire.

He understood now why his parents had acted strangely unconcerned about his narrow escape from Black Bear Mountain.

With his dad a photographer and his mother a writer, both working on a magazine article about the event, they had known all along the movie was being filmed in the area. But just like so many of the inn-keepers, restaurant owners and local officials who served the visiting filmmakers during their short stay in the area, his parents, too, had been sworn to secrecy.

It all seemed surreal now. Witnessing part of a movie being filmed in Eagle Bay? Your cat taking off with a raccoon on a hot air balloon ride? Sharing laughs and popcorn at the Strand with a famous actor?

To my new friend, Justin,
Mack Carson

As the days had gone by, if it weren't for that personal note and signature on the poster as a constant reminder, it would have been a lot harder to believe any of it had really happened at all.

Dax jumped up on the bed and Justin stroked her head and neck.

There had been a rematch earlier in the day at the golf course. Nick had insisted on the contest, hoping to remove what he now called, the golf *curse*. Once again, Justin had won the game, which meant he also earned the right to choose what special activity he and his friends did the next day.

Even after seeing firsthand how something can seem real, but be pretend, poor Nick simply could not stop believing that flying monkeys were haunting the trees above the seventh hole. He just kept waiting for them to swoop down on him.

But Nick's disappointment at losing the match did not last very long. Justin beamed as he recalled the smile on his friend's face when he announced his final decision. Tomorrow? They would go fishing!

This has to be best summer ever, he thought. *It can't get any better.*

Of course, he thought that every year.

DAX FACTS

Children's Books set in the Adirondacks

Did you know the *Hardy Boys* and *Nancy Drew* have visited the Adirondacks?

When we first began writing The Adirondack Kids® series, we thought it might be fun to start a collection of other children's books set in the Adirondacks. After all, how many could here be?

We were surprised to learn there have been many children's books published that are set in this region we love, and our small collection quickly grew from just a few books to nearly 100!

The Go Ahead Boys, *The Motorcycle Chums*, *The Nowaday Girls*, *The Screech Owls*, the *Girl Scouts* and even *The Boxcar Children* are also among those who have had adventures in the Adirondacks in books published nearly every decade from the late 1800's until our own day. And at least one book for young people, *Cold River*, featuring the characters Tim and Lizzy Allison, fighting to survive in the frozen Adirondack wilderness, was also made into a major motion picture.

Our guess is as we keep searching, we'll find even more Adirondack titles to be added to the shelves of our personal library at home.

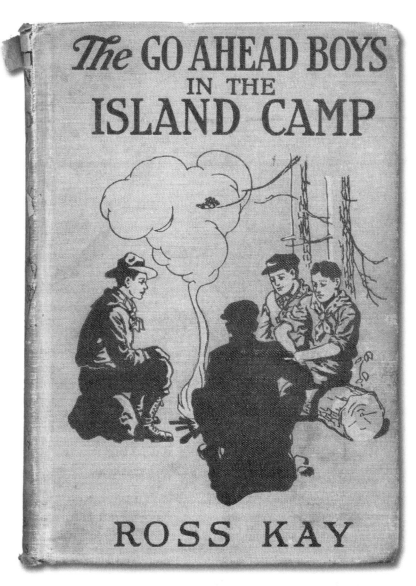

The Go Ahead Boys in the Island Camp by Ross Kay was published nearly 100 years ago, and is one of dozens of children's books over three centuries set in the Adirondacks. This book was originally published by Barse & Hopkins in 1916.

The Coyote

Sometimes called a coydog or brush dog, the **coyote** can be found throughout the Adirondacks. The species began to arrive in the 1920's to 1930's and was well established by the middle of the 20th century.

Even though coyotes in the Adirondacks tend to be larger than those found anywhere in all of North America, they are still smaller than wolves. The main color of their fur may be gray or red or yellow-brown, and they sport limp, but bushy tails.

Their sharply pointed ears and pointed noses help them hear and smell to hunt other animals for food, although they do love berries in the summer. Coyotes are wary – are most active at dawn, at dusk and at night – and are often mistaken for dogs. As a result, they are not often seen by humans. But they can often be identified by campers at twighlight, howling.

Coyote. Photography ©2008 Eric Dresser

The envelope of this hot air balloon features characters from *The Wizard of Oz*! Photography ©2008 Gary VanRiper

DAX FACTS

Adirondack Balloon Festival

The **Adirondack Balloon Festival**, is held the third full weekend each September at the Floyd Bennett Memorial Airport in the Glens Falls/Queensbury area of New York state. For more than 35 years the event has attracted thousands of onlookers to celebrate and enjoy the spectacular sights and flights of hot air balloons.

The large portion of the balloon with colorful patterns or pictures, and sometimes of unique shape, is called an envelope. At 5 a.m., the envelopes are filled with hot air and one by one, the large wicker baskets carrying the pilots and passengers begin lifting into the sky.

Lake George, New York hosts the Moon Glow portion of the Festival, with tethered balloons aglow near the lake at night, followed by a grand fireworks display.

There is no admission charge to enter the festival.

For additional information on the Adirondack Balloon Festival, contact the Lake George Chamber of Commerce at www.visitlakegeorge.com.

About the Authors

Gary and Justin VanRiper are a father-and-son writing team residing in Camden, New York, with their family and cat, Dax. They spend many summer and autumn days at camp on Fourth Lake in the Adirondacks.

The Adirondack Kids® began as a writing exercise at home when Justin was in third grade. Encouraged after a public reading of an early draft at a Parents As Reading Partners (PARP) program in their school district, the project grew into a middle-reader chapter book series.

The Adirondack Kids® #5 – Islands in the Sky, won the 2005–06 Adirondack Literary Award for Best Children's Book. Books in the series appear regularly on the New York State Charlotte Award's Suggested Summer Reading List.

Authors Justin and Gary VanRiper often visit elementary schools to encourage students to read and write.
Photography ©2008 Carol VanRiper

About the Illustrators

Carol McCurn VanRiper lives and works in Camden, New York. She is also the wife and mother, respectively, of *The Adirondack Kids*® co-authors, Gary and Justin VanRiper. She inherited the job as publicist when *The Adirondack Kids*® grew from a family dream into a small publishing company. Her black and white interior illustrations appear in *The Adirondack Kids*®, books #4 – #8.

Susan Loeffler is a freelance illustrator who lives in upstate New York. Her full-color cover illustrations appear in *The Adirondack Kids*® books #1 – #8; *The Adirondack Kids*® poster; and on the cover of *The Adirondack Kids*® coloring book, *Runaway Dax*, which also features her interior black and white illustrations.

Co-author Gary VanRiper and illustrator Susan Loeffler review sketches. Photography ©2008 Carol VanRiper

The Adirondack Kids® #1

Justin Robert is ten years old and likes computers, biking and peanut butter cups. But his passion is animals. When an uncommon pair of Common Loons takes up residence on Fourth Lake near the family camp, he will do anything he can to protect them.

The Adirondack Kids® #2
Rescue on Bald Mountain

Justin Robert and Jackie Salsberry are on a special mission. It is Fourth of July weekend in the Adirondacks and time for the annual ping-pong ball drop at Inlet. Their best friend, Nick Barnes, has won the opportunity to release the balls from a seaplane, but there is just one problem. He is afraid of heights. With a single day remaining before the big event, Justin and Jackie decide there is only one way to help Nick overcome his fear. Climb Bald Mountain!

All on sale wherever great books on the Adirondacks are found.

The **Adirondack Kids**® #3
The Lost Lighthouse

Justin Robert, Jackie Salsberry and Nick Barnes are fishing under sunny Adirondack skies when a sudden and violent storm chases them off Fourth Lake and into an unfamiliar forest – a forest that has harbored a secret for more than 100 years.

The **Adirondack Kids**® #4
The Great Train Robbery

It's all aboard the train at the North Creek station, and word is out there are bandits in the region. Will the train be robbed? Justin Robert and Jackie Salsberry are excited. Nick Barnes is bored – but he won't be for long.

Also available on **The Adirondack Kids**® official web site
www.ADIRONDACKKIDS.com
Watch for more adventures of The Adirondack Kids® *coming soon.*

The Adirondack Kids® #5
Islands in the Sky

Justin Robert, Jackie Salsberry and Nick Barnes head for the Adirondack high peaks wilderness while Justin's calico cat, Dax, embarks on an unexpected tour of the Adirondack Park.

The Adirondack Kids® #6
Secret of the Skeleton Key

While preparing their pirate ship for the Anything That Floats Race, Justin and Nick discover an antique bottle riding the waves on Fourth Lake. Inside the bottle is a key that leads The Adirondack Kids to unlock an old camp mystery.

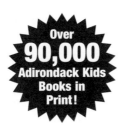

Over **90,000** Adirondack Kids Books in Print!

Also available on **The Adirondack Kids®** official web site

www.ADIRONDACKKIDS.com

Watch for more adventures of The Adirondack Kids® coming soon.

ᵗʰᵉ**Adirondack Kids® #7**
Mystery of the
Missing Moose

Justin Robert has the camera. Nick Barnes has the binoculars. And Jackie Salsberry has the common sense! The Adirondack Kids are led into a series of unexpected encounters with local wildlife as they search Eagle Bay for any sign of a missing moose!

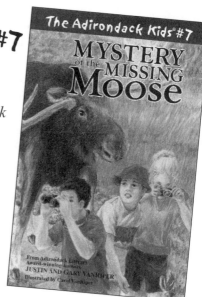

ᵗʰᵉ**Adirondack Kids® #8**
Escape from
Black Bear Mountain

Justin Robert wants to climb all of the mountains near his family's Fourth Lake camp before the summer is over. Jackie Salsberry can't wait to join him. Nick Barnes would rather go fishing. Next on the list is Black Bear Mountain. An easy hike, right? If only they had noticed the **Trail Closed** *sign before they took off together!*

Also available on **The Adirondack Kids®** official web site
www.ADIRONDACKKIDS.com
Watch for more adventures of The Adirondack Kids® coming soon.

The **Adirondack Kids**®
Story & Coloring Book
Runaway Dax

Artist Susan Loeffler brings a favorite Adirondack Kids® character – Dax – to life in 32 coloring book illustrations set to a storyline for young readers written by Adirondack Kids® co-creator and author, Justin VanRiper.

The **Adirondack Kids**® **Wall Poster**

17" x 22" – Full Color
Features Justin, Nick, Jackie and Dax in the Adirondack Mountains. Also featured are a black bear, pileated woodpecker and red admiral butterflies, all creatures of the Adirondacks.

Also available on **The Adirondack Kids**® official web site
www.ADIRONDACKKIDS.com
Watch for more adventures of The Adirondack Kids® coming soon.

Watch for more adventures
of The Adirondack Kids® coming soon.